PENGUIN & MOOSE
Brave the Night

Written by Hannah C. Hall • Illustrated by Stacy Curtis

For Mom the Fearless and Dad the Brave. —H.H.

 In memory of Jodi Borger. —S.C.

ISBN: 978-1-5460-1508-6

WorthyKids
Hachette Book Group
1290 Avenue of the Americas
New York, NY 10104

Library of Congress Cataloging-in-Publication Data
Names: Hall, Hannah C., author. | Curtis, Stacy, illustrator.
Title: Penguin & Moose brave the night / written by Hannah C. ; illustrated by Stacy Curtis.
Other titles: Penguin and Moose brave the night
Description: New York, NY : WorthyKids, [2021] | Audience: Ages 4-8. | Summary: "Penguin goes to his first sleepover at his friend Moose's house, but Penguin is afraid of the dark. Penguin finds creative ways to protect himself, but when nothing works Moose shares his own trick: remembering that God is always with him"— Provided by publisher.
Identifiers: LCCN 2020037039 | ISBN 9781546015086 (hardcover)
Subjects: CYAC: Sleepovers—Fiction. | Fear of the dark—Fiction. | Penguins—Fiction. | Moose—Fiction. | Christian life—Fiction.
Classification: LCC PZ7.H1444 Pe 2021 | DDC [E]—dc23
LC record available at https://lccn.loc.gov/2020037039

Designed by Eve DeGrie

Printed and bound in China
APS
10 9 8 7 6 5 4 3 2 1

PENGUIN

was thrilled.

Completely, undeniably, tingly-to-his-toes thrilled.

Moose had invited him to spend the night.
He'd never spent the night at a friend's house before.

MOOSE
answered the door in his PJs.
"What should we do first?"

Penguin had a few ideas.
"Pillow fight? Popcorn? Pillow *fort*?"

Moose agreed.

"And Mama promised us
a bedtime story too."

Penguin's flippers stiffened.

Bedtime story?
Bedtime stories meant bedtime.
And bedtime meant nighttime.
And nighttime meant
Lights. Out. Time.

Penguin was glad he'd come prepared.
He'd packed only the essentials.

That night, after Moose's favorite *Super Penguin* storybook and Mrs. M's snug-as-a-bug bedtime hugs, Penguin zip, zip, zipped himself into his sleeping bag.

"Moose, where's your night-light?"

"I don't have one." Moose gave his pillow a fluff.
"But Mama always turns the hall light on."

Penguin's feathers
prickled.

Hall lights were **absolutely not**
the same as night–lights. Not even close.

Penguin tried squeezing his eyes shut extra tight and pretending there was a night-light, but that just made it extra dark.

He tried sleeping with his eyes open, but that just made his eyeballs scratchy.

"Moose,"
Penguin whispered loudly.
"I can't sleep."

Moose snuggled deep in his covers.
"Mama says when I can't sleep
to close my eyes and think about happy things.
Like fishing or sledding or a nice, fresh salad."

Moose switched on his lamp. "And you'd probably feel sleepier if you took off the helmet."

Penguin didn't think so.
"But what if I need head protection?"

"In bed?" Moose considered.
"I usually only wear a helmet on my bike."

Moose had a point. Penguin slipped off the helmet.
It was considerably comfier without it.
But not quite all-the-way comfy.
Not yet.

"This pillow's tickling my face feathers." Penguin squinted.
No wonder. It had **words** stitched across it:

"So do not fear,
for I am with you."

Penguin's beak scrunched.
Who said anything about
being **afraid?**

He flipped the pillow over.

"Now it's all lumpy and bumpy."
He gave the pillow a punch.

Then a couple more.

Moose frowned. "I've never noticed any lumps before. It's my softest one."

Penguin fished his flipper inside the pillowcase.

"I guess it could be my **slingshot** that's the problem," said Penguin.
"I stuck it in here with a couple of rocks, just to be safe."

"Safe from what?"

"Intruders, of course! I've got pretty good aim
if my target holds totally, entirely, perfectly still.
Do you think gigantic killer bees ever hold still?"

"Penguin," Moose said softly.
"You don't need to be scared here."

"I'm not scared."
Penguin's voice trembled. "Not even a little bit."

"Oh." Moose was thoughtful.
"I used to be, especially at night.
But I'm not anymore.
Pop says that God
is always with me.

"Even when I'm sleeping." Moose yawned. "Pop even stitched it on my pillowcase, to help me not forget."

Penguin huffed. Tickly pillowcase words wouldn't do much good against a swarm of humongous penguin-snatching-sized killer bees.

But **bug spray** would.

Fortunately, Penguin had packed a can or two in his backpack,
just in case he missed the bees with his slingshot.
Unlikely, but possible.

He unzip, –zip, –zipped
his sleeping bag
and climbed out.

Crick. Crack. CRUNCH!

"Yowwww!"

Penguin had stepped on something hard.
And pokey. And booby-trappy.
And an awful lot like the hard, pokey
building blocks he'd booby-trapped
the floor around his
sleeping bag with.

Hot tears dribbled down Penguin's beak.

He was tired and his feet hurt and none of his plans were working and Moose was snoring and there was nothing left to do but be scared and scratchy-eyeballed all by himself.

Wait a minute. Moose was snoring?
Without a night–light? Or booby traps?
Or a single, solitary weapon?
That was impossible! Wasn't it?

Then Penguin remembered.
Moose was asleep because
Moose wasn't afraid.

And if Moose's pillowcase was right,
and Penguin was never really alone—
even at night, even at Moose's house—
then maybe **Penguin didn't
need to be afraid either.**

Penguin yawned and zip, zip, zipped himself back in.
Being a scaredy-penguin was exhausting anyway.

And it required way too much packing.

The light was bright outside
when Penguin and Moose
woke the next morning.

Penguin grinned.

He'd survived, and he hadn't ended up needing the
night-light or the slingshot or the bug spray or anything.

Except for the **helmet**, that is.

Which ended up coming in pretty handy after all.